JOURNEY TO THE FROZEN PLANET

An Early Chapter Book

Based on the episode written by **Sascha Paladino**

Adapted by **Sheila Sweeny Higginson**

SUSTAINABLE
FORESTRY
INITIATIVE
Certified Sourcing
www.sfiprogram.org
SFI-01415

DISNEP PRESS
Los Angeles • New York

HOME, STELLAR HOME

CAPTAIN'S LOG

ALL IS CLEAR ON THE *STELLOSPHERE.*
THE SHIP IS SET ON A STEADY COURSE.
OUR CREW HAS PLENTY OF TIME FOR
RECREATIONAL ACTIVITIES, BOTH ON
AND OFF THE SHIP.

—PHOEBE CALLISTO

SPACETASTIC FACT

There are at least one hundred billion galaxies in the universe. How many do you think we'll get to explore?

I'm Miles, and I'm the luckiest kid in the universe: my home, school, and playground are all in outer space! That makes me a space adventurer.

SPACETASTIC FACT

The word *astronaut* comes from two Greek words that together mean "star sailor."

My family works for the TTA. That's short for the Tomorrowland Transit Authority. We help out with anything that has to do with space transportation, like repairing spacecraft and meeting aliens!

Check out my home, the *Stellosphere*. It's a floating spaceship designed just for my family!

THE BRIDGE

This is the nerve center of the *Stellosphere*—and the place you can usually find Mom. We use our Operation Station to gather all the information we need for our missions.

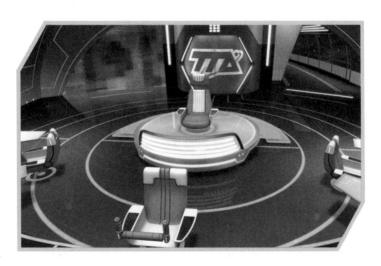

LIVING ROOM

The ship has a gravity generator installed under the floor. When the blue floor lights are on, that means the gravity is activated.

MY ROOM

Check out my room. It's pretty stellar, right?

KITCHEN

This is our kitchen. Stella, our ship's computer, can make food. But my parents cook, too.

BIO-GARDEN

This is kind of like our backyard. We grow all kinds of things here, even fruits and vegetables! It's also a great place to play catch with Merc.

Look what I found! It's an old model kit. I found it in Dad's workshop. He said we could put it together.

Now I just have to find Loretta!

PICKING UP THE PIECES

Merc and I find Loretta at
our dining table, looking at her
BraceLex. Usually, Loretta knows
everything about everything. But
this little box has got even my
genius sister stumped!

"What is it?" Loretta asks when I show her the box.

"Aroooo?" Merc wonders.

"It's called a bicycle," I tell her. "Dad said they used them back on Earth. Before they had Blastboards."

I can't imagine life without my Blastboard!

Loretta and I examine the box. "Weird," we both say at the same time.

I guess brothers and sisters think alike.

SPACETASTIC FACT

A bicycle is one of the most efficient vehicles ever invented by humans.

I dump the pieces on the table. Then I start to put them together. It seems pretty easy.

SPACETASTIC FACT

The Outer Space Treaty was signed in 1967. It is the basis for all international space law.

Loretta thinks we should follow the instructions. She always follows the rules. I think I like it better *my* way.

"Miles, that's not right!" Loretta cries when I move a wheel. "That's not how it looks on the box!"

Dad interrupts us with a plate of his famous antigravity pancakes.

"Hey, cool your boosters, kiddos," he says.

"My boosters are cool," Loretta replies.

Dad tells us to remember:

COSMIC EXPLORER RULE NUMBER

SOME MISSIONS CALL FOR INSTRUCTIONS. SOMETIMES YOU HAVE TO FIND YOUR OWN WAY.

SPACETASTIC FACT

The first earthling to go into outer space ate food from a toothpaste-like tube. Yuck! Antigravity pancakes are so much better.

CALLING ALL TTA CREW

"Attention!" Stella, our ship's artificial intelligence, says. "The Tomorrowland Transit Authority is calling."

Loretta and I gobble down the last of the antigravity pancakes. Then we head to the bridge.

Mom is already sitting at the holo-screen.

"Callisto family, reporting for duty," she tells the admirals.

The TTA admirals are Watson and Crick. They're two heads on one alien body. I know, it sounds strange. But remember, we *are* in outer space.

"We've recently found a new exoplanet called Thurio," Watson reports.

If you're wondering what an exoplanet is, join the club. I don't know what it is, either.

"An exoplanet is any planet outside of our solar system that orbits a star much like our sun," Watson explains.

SPACETASTIC FACT
Did you know the earthling scientists James Watson and Francis Crick helped discover the structure of DNA, the building block of all life?

Watson tells us that there may be hundreds of billions of exoplanets in our galaxy. That's a lot!

"And this one is icy and cold," Crick adds.

The TTA sent a rover to Thurio to take measurements. It froze.

Now we have a new mission. We have to travel to Thurio. We have to thaw out the rover and bring it back.

Even better, we get fancy new upgrades to our QuestComs.

Our QuestComs are endlessly upgradable personal tech devices. We wear them on our wrists. Now we're getting heat rays.

"Stand by for upgrade transmission," Watson tells us.

"Standing by," we all reply.

SPACETASTIC FACT

A laser doesn't have a temperature, but the most powerful one can heat matter to over 3.6 million degrees!

In just a few seconds, we all have heat rays on our QuestComs. I love getting new technology from the TTA! I can't wait to try this one out.

Loretta pulls up the instructions for the new heat rays. "We'll learn how to use our upgrades before we start blasting," she says.

I don't think we need all those instructions. Don't we just point the heat ray at the thing we want to melt?

"Admirals, we'll get that rover out of the ice before you can say *hyperspace*," Mom promises.

"Best of luck, Callistos," Watson says.

"And try not to freeze your eyebrows off," Crick adds. "It's hard to get them back on!"

SPACETASTIC FACT

Light speed is more than 186,000 miles per second. Travel in hyperspace is even faster!

THE FAMILY RIDE

Mom leads the way to our StarJetter. It's a small ship. We use it to explore places where the *Stellosphere* can't land.

Everyone puts on a space suit. Then we climb inside.

3 . . . 2 . . . 1 . . .
BLAST OFF!

"Leo, engage landing gear," Mom tells Dad when we get close to the planet.

"Will do," Dad replies. "This one is going to be smooth."

The StarJetter hovers over Thurio.

Before even setting foot on this new planet, we have to do some research. While Dad lands the StarJetter, Mom and Loretta read up on Thurio.

SPACETASTIC FACT
Space suits have to protect astronauts from extreme temperatures and help them breathe. There's no air in space!

29

"Make sure to activate your thermal shields," Mom reminds us.

"And don't forget," Dad adds, "Thurio is made almost completely of ice."

Loretta studies a map of Thurio. She sees something weird.

"There's actually a river here," she informs us. "It's some kind of salt liquid."

"Look out for that river," Mom says. "And remember, it's really slippery out there. So watch your step."

SPACETASTIC FACT
The Nile is the longest river on Earth, but the Amazon contains more water.

ON NOT-SO-THIN ICE

5

Merc, our robo-ostrich, jumps down the stairs first.

He didn't listen to Mom. He slips on the frozen surface of Thurio and slides down a hill.

Luckily, the hill isn't too big. Merc slowly slides to a stop right in front of something interesting. . . .

SPACETASTIC FACT
The planet Uranus is made of ice.

"Hey, Merc already found the rover," Mom says. "That was fast!"

"Nice work, Merc!" I cheer.

I'm so proud of my best friend. He may not be 100 percent perfect, but he always comes through for the family. Merc is the best mechanical emotionally responsive ostrich ever!

I hear the sound of something sliding toward us and turn around. It's Dad on his laser skis!

"Thurio may be cold, but it's got some sweet slopes!" Dad says.

SPACETASTIC FACT

The surface temperature of Uranus, the coldest planet in our solar system, can get to be -216 degrees Celsius.

"Now let's get this puppy out of here!" says Dad.

When we're on a mission, everyone has a job to do. Since Mom's the captain, she gives us our assignments.

"Miles, Loretta," Mom says, "you defrost the rover."

We're on it like a comet!

We'll need a flat surface to pull the rover to the StarJetter.

Mom and Dad lay down a hard light-track while we focus on the rover.

SPACETASTIC FACT

Scientists have found twenty-seven moons orbiting Uranus.

FOLLOW THE LEADER

Loretta and I have to figure out how to get our heat rays to work best.

She starts to read the instructions.

"It says to turn the gamma splitter to 391 for five picoseconds, then lower the sonic tachyogram for eight nanoseconds, then . . ."

Ugh! There must be a faster way.

SPACETASTIC FACT
A nanosecond is one-billionth of a second.

Loretta is still focused on the instructions. But I'm not like my sister. I don't like to always play it by the book.

I look around for inspiration. Then I notice Merc's wings. That's it! Now I have a great idea! We can use Merc's rocket boosters to melt the ice.

Merc curls his wings into rockets. He fires them up. He turns around. The heat starts to melt the ice.

"It's working!" I cheer.

I knew we could do this without any instructions. I found my own way, just like Dad said.

SPACETASTIC FACT

NASA's Mars rover *Curiosity* was named by a sixth grader.

Loretta turns around and sees Merc melting the ice. Her eyes open wide. I can tell from the way she's looking at us that she's not a big fan of my innovative idea.

SPACETASTIC FACT

Rockets work by burning either liquid or solid fuel. The hot gases expand and stream out the back of the rocket, pushing it in the opposite direction.

"Miles!" she yells. "I thought we were using the heat rays."

"But this way works, too," I say.

"Well, I'm following the instructions," Loretta replies. "And I cannot concentrate with all this noise."

Loretta has a point. Merc's rocket boosters *are* noisy. But I have a point, too. They are working.

Loretta shakes her head and sighs. She doesn't want to listen to me. Why can't she see that I just want to find a quicker, better way to do things? This is one of those times when we're not thinking alike at all.

When Loretta starts to walk away, I feel my brother-worry senses kick into action, and I remember Mom's advice.

"Be careful, Loretta," I call. "It's really slippery out there!"

"I'm always careful!" Loretta shouts back.

That's usually true. Loretta is careful, and she explores on her own a lot. But most of the planets we visit aren't covered in ice. I hope she'll be okay.

A TOUGH BREAK

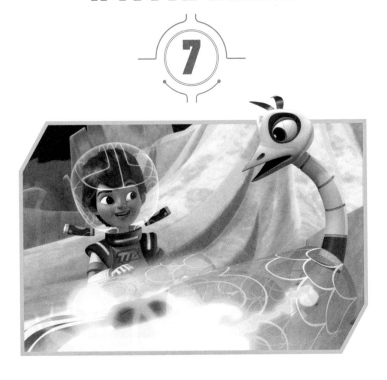

I would follow Loretta, but we still have a rover to retrieve.

Flames blaze from Merc's wings. They surround the ice that's covering the rover. Merc is doing a spacetastic job melting the ice with his rocket boosters.

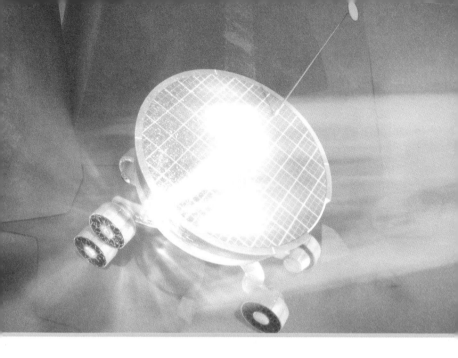

He sure is hot stuff! I bet we'll have this finished before Loretta comes back. Wait until she hears that we did this without instructions!

"Keep it up, buddy," I tell him.

SPACETASTIC FACT
Scientists can learn about the history of a planet by studying its ice.

CRACK!

The ice is open! Merc did it! That's twice in a row that he's helped on this mission. Just one more reason Merc is the best robo-pet ever.

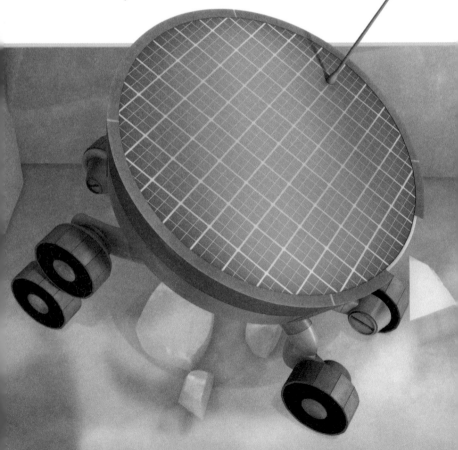

I wish Loretta could see this. . . .
She's been gone for a while.
I thought she'd have finished
reading the instructions by now.

Oh, well. I'm sure she'll come
back soon with a ton of new
information stored on her BraceLex.

SPACETASTIC FACT
NASA rocket launches can be so loud
that scientists have to make sure they
don't knock over buildings.

WHOAAA

SPACETASTIC FACT

There is no weather in space. It takes an atmosphere to create weather. An atmosphere is like a blanket of gases that surrounds a planet.

Mom and Dad have finished laying down the light-track and come to check on us.

"Where's Loretta?" Mom asks.

"Loretta? Come in, Loretta," I call into my QuestCom.

Loretta doesn't answer.

Mom tries calling Loretta, too.

"Her QuestCom is off," Mom tells us.

Dad's worried. Loretta knows:

COSMIC EXPLORER RULE NUMBER

NEVER TURN OFF YOUR QUESTCOM.

Something is wrong. Very wrong.

SPACETASTIC FACT
Ice cracks can be formed by wind, waves, and temperature changes in an ice sheet.

RESCUE MISSION

We have to get the rover to the
StarJetter. But that will have to
wait. . . .

"We need to find your sister,"
Mom says.

"On it, Mom!" I reply.

Mom pulls up a map of Thurio on her QuestCom.

"Miles, Merc, you head south," she tells us. "Honey, scan the north quadrant," she says to Dad. "I'll check the eastern slopes."

SPACETASTIC FACT

A "frost quake," or the booming sound of cracking ice, is known as a cryoseism.

"Be careful, everyone," Dad advises us.

Got it, Dad.

Merc and I hold each other as we slide down Thurio's icy slopes. This might be fun if I wasn't so worried about Loretta.

Then Merc sees something in the distance.

"Aroooo-ooooo!" he says.

(In case you don't speak robo-ostrich, that means "Check it out!")

SPACETASTIC FACT

Astronomers use high-powered telescopes to learn about the universe. There are telescopes on Earth's surface and orbiting Earth in space.

SPACETASTIC FACT

Emergency flares contain magnesium, so they can't be put out by water—or melting ice!

It's an emergency flare that looks like a giant glowing arrow in the sky. Loretta must have fired it.

"That must be her!" I yell to Merc. "Come on!"

I let Mom and Dad know that we have a lock on Loretta.

"We'll follow your signal," Mom says.

SPACETASTIC FACT
Our solar system is trillions of miles wide.

Merc and I zip and zoom across the ice. Soon I see my sister at the bottom of an ice slide.

"Loretta! We're coming!" I shout.

She looks up and waves to us.

REUNITED?

Loretta is really happy to see me. She followed the directions, of course. They told her what to do in case of emergency. That's how she found the flare button on the side of her space suit.

SPACETASTIC FACT

Orbit means to travel around.
A planet orbits a star.

"It's like Dad said," Loretta says. "Some missions call for instructions. And *I* read 'em."

I reach down to help my sister out of the ice slide. But when Loretta reaches for my hand, the ice starts to crack. Before I can grab her, she's swept away on an ice floe!

Mom and Dad arrive just in time.

"Don't worry, starshine!" Mom yells. "We'll save you!"

Dad finds an icicle and holds it out.

"Grab this!" he says to Loretta. She misses.

SPACETASTIC FACT

Icicles form when water freezes as it drips off an object.

I hop on my Blastboard. I try
to reach Loretta, but I can't. She's
bouncing around like a pinball in
the icy river.

A CHANGE OF PLANS

Loretta likes to follow instructions. That's great—until you get stuck on a piece of ice speeding down a river on a freezing exoplanet.

There aren't any instructions for what to do when that happens.

"WATERFALL!" Loretta screams. She's heading right toward it.

SPACETASTIC FACT
On Earth, ice floes can be giant— more than six miles across!

It's time for some quick thinking. Loretta lucked out. She has a little brother who isn't so good at following directions but is excellent at coming up with great ideas on the fly.

All I have with me is my Blastboard, my zip line, and my laserang. And I need to get Loretta off that ice floe and onto solid ground.

Plan A was the icicle. Plan B was my Blastboard. Now it's time for Plan C.

SPACETASTIC FACT

There have been more than three hundred manned space missions since the first one in 1961.

I fly to the other side of the river and flip my Blastboard so it stops and sticks in the ice. Then I hit my belt buckle to activate my zip line.

"Dad, catch!" I call.

"Miles!" Loretta yells. "This is no time to play catch!"

I pull out my zip line. It shoots across the river. Dad catches it and ties his end to a chunk of ice.
I secure my end to my Blastboard.

I pull my laserang out of my backpack. I wind up and throw.

"Loretta!" I call. "Grab it!"

Loretta leaps up and catches it. Then she rides the zip line to shore, safe and sound.

SPACETASTIC FACT
Humans have been using skis to travel across the ice for thousands of years.

SPACETASTIC FACT

The source of a river can be a lake,
several small streams coming together,
or melting snow.

GO YOUR OWN WAY

What a spacetastic rescue! I ride my Blastboard over the river and land next to my family. Finally, we're all back together again.

"Now that's what I like to see, Callistos!" Mom cheers.

Loretta hands me my laserang. "Thanks, Miles," she says. "There were definitely not instructions for how to do that."

That's why I had to make up my own way.

I think it's time for a new mission: get off this exoplanet and warm up with some comet cocoa (after we get the rover)!

When we get home to the *Stellosphere*, Loretta and I go back to building the bicycle.

"Let's build the model your way," I tell Loretta. "It's like Dad said, some missions call for instructions."

"But you made it look really cool your way," says Loretta. "Different, but cool."

SPACETASTIC FACT
Zip lines work with a simple machine—a pulley!

Just then, Merc barrels in. He
stumbles toward his cocoa but
misses the mark. Model parts fly
everywhere!

Or we could make the bicycle Merc's way.

What do you think?

SPACETASTIC FACT

The oldest boomerang ever found was made from a mammoth tusk.

COSMIC EXPLORER RULE NUMBER

NEVER TURN OFF YOUR QUESTCOM.

COSMIC EXPLORER RULE NUMBER

SOME MISSIONS CALL FOR INSTRUCTIONS. SOMETIMES YOU HAVE TO FIND YOUR OWN WAY.